Walking Round the Garden

A Red Fox Book

Published by Random House Children's Books
20 Vauxhall Bridge Road, London SW1V 2SA

A division of The Random House Group Ltd
London Melbourne Sydney Auckland
Johannesburg and agencies throughout the world

1 3 5 7 9 10 8 6 4 2

First published in Great Britain by The Bodley Head Children's Books 1997

Red Fox edition 2001

Printed and bound in Singapore

THE RANDOM HOUSE GROUP Limited Reg. No. 954009

www.randomhouse.co.uk

ISBN 0 09 926283 5

Walking Round the Garden

the Garden

JOHN PRATER

RED FOX

Walking round

he garden,

Like

teddy bear,

One step

wo steps,

Tickle you

under there.

Walking dowr

he hallway,

Up and up

he stairs,

One step

wo steps,

What c

clever bear!

Sitting in

he bedroom,

What a

leepy ted,

All I need i

a goodnight kiss

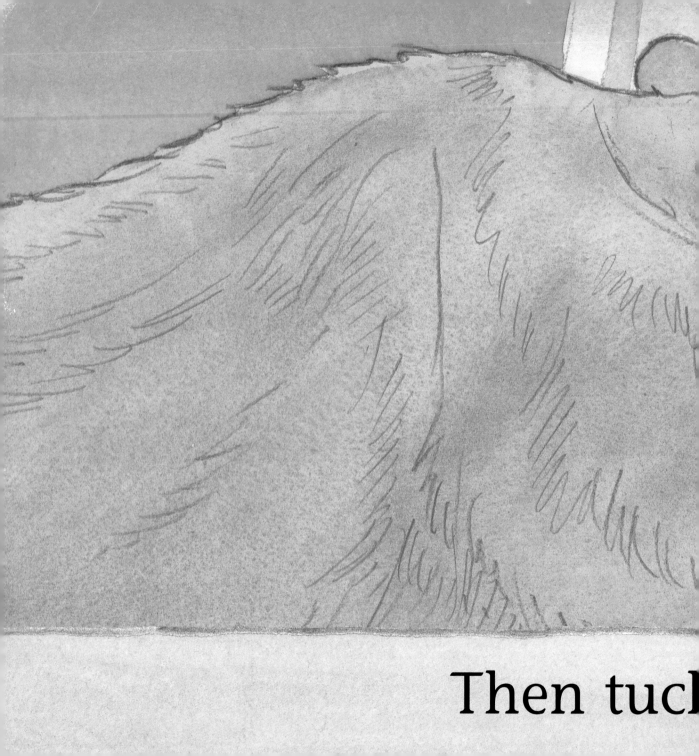

Then tuck

you into bed.

Other Baby Bear books to collect:

Again!

Clap Your Hands

I'm Coming to Get You!

The Bear Went Over the Mountain

Oh Where, Oh Where?

Number One, Tickle Your Tum